The Giraffe and the Pelly and Me

LEVEL 3

Re-told by: Kathryn Harper
Series Editor: Melanie Williams

Pearson Education Limited
Edinburgh Gate, Harlow,
Essex CM20 2JE, England
and Associated Companies throughout the world.

ISBN: 978-1-4479-3133-1

This edition first published by Pearson Education Ltd 2014

1 3 5 7 9 10 8 6 4 2

Set in 17/21pt OT Fiendstar
Printed in China
SWTC/01

Published by Pearson Education Ltd in association with
Penguin Books Ltd, a Penguin Random House company.

For a complete list of the titles available in the Penguin Kids series please go to www.penguinreaders.com.
Alternatively, write to your local Pearson Education office or to: Penguin Readers Marketing Department,
Pearson Education, Edinburgh Gate, Harlow, Essex CM20 2JE, England.

In my town, there is an old white house. People do not live in the house now. It is dirty and closed.

But many years ago, it was The Grubber – a sweet shop, mmmm... a beautiful sweet shop.

I would like my own sweet shop. I dream about my own Grubber shop. It has a lot of sweets. There are sweets in red boxes, sweets in blue boxes and sweets in small bags.

My own sweet shop!

One day, I walk by The Grubber.
The window is open.

A bath flies out of the window.

CRASH!

And then a toilet and a sink!

CRASH! CRASH! CRASH!

'Who's there?' I shout.

There is no answer.

The next day, I go to The Grubber.

It is different. There is a new door. It is red and very TALL.

There are also some new words on the window.

I try to read them ...
Window Cleaning.

I see a head in one window. Then a different window opens.

'I'm Pelly,' a white bird with an orange beak says. 'This is Giraffe. Her legs are at the bottom of the house and her head's at the top!'

Then a window on the first floor opens. It's a dancing and singing monkey –

'We are the window cleaners we three,

The Giraffe, the Pelly and me!

We don't use ladders, not we,

The Giraffe, the Pelly and me!'

I jump into Pelly's beak. We fly up to Giraffe.

'What's your name?' Giraffe asks.

'Billy,' I say.

'Please help us,' Giraffe says. 'We need a job. We're hungry. Monkey eats nuts. Pelly eats fish and I eat **purple** flowers!'

A big car stops and a man comes to the door.

'That's the Duke's car,' I say. 'He's a
VERY IMPORTANT MAN.'

'I've got a letter from the Duke,'
the man says.

He then reads, ' "I'm looking for window cleaners. My house is very big and there are hundreds of dirty windows. Please come quickly." '

'Thank you,' Giraffe says. 'We're coming right now.'

We arrive at the Duke's house.

'Look at those windows!' Monkey cries. 'What a lot to do!'

It is time for work! Quickly, Monkey puts water in Pelly's beak. Then Monkey jumps on Giraffe's head.

'Bring the water to the fourth floor, Pelly,' Giraffe says.

'That's very high,' the Duke says.

'Duke,' Giraffe says. 'It's not high for me!'

Monkey dances on Giraffe's head and her neck grows **longer** ...

and **longer** ...
and **higher** ...
and **higher** ...

Now Giraffe's head is at the fourth floor windows and Pelly flies up with the water. They smile and clean the windows.

Pelly, Monkey and Giraffe stop.
They do not move.

'What's wrong?' the Duke asks.

'There's a thief in the room,'
Giraffe says to the Duke
quietly. 'He's taking some
jewels.'

'STOP HIM! STOP HIM!'
the Duke shouts.

Pelly quickly flies up through the window.

After a minute he comes out of the window and his beak is very big.

'He's got him!' Monkey cries. 'Pelly's got the thief in his beak!'

'Good work!' the Duke says.

NEEE-NAWWW!

NEEE-NAWWW!

NEEE-NAWWW!

A noisy police car with six policemen arrives.

'The thief is in Pelly's big orange beak,' the Duke says. 'Ready? One, two, three! Open up, Pelly.'

Pelly opens his beak and the policemen take the thief out.

'WOW! Look at all the jewels,' a policeman says.

The Duke smiles at us.

'Those jewels are very important to me,' the Duke says. 'Thank you, Pelly, Giraffe, Monkey and Billy. You are great!'

We smile at the Duke.

'Giraffe, Pelly and Monkey, you can come and live here,' the Duke says.

'Thank you, Duke,' Giraffe says. 'But there is one small problem. We are very hungry and we need ...'

'That isn't a problem! *I* know what you need,' the Duke says. 'Giraffe, you need purple flowers, Monkey needs nuts and Pelly needs fish!'

Soon, Giraffe is eating purple flowers, Monkey is eating nuts in a tree and Pelly is eating fish from the river.

'And you, Billy,' the Duke says. 'What would you like?'

'There's an old house,' I say. 'It was The Grubber –
a sweet shop.'

'A SWEET SHOP!' the Duke shouts. 'You would like your
own sweet shop. OK, let's buy it!'

Soon, men are working at the shop. They are making shelves for the sweets.

Then sweet boxes arrive. There are sweets in red boxes, sweets in blue boxes and sweets in small bags.

My own sweet shop!

After a fun first day in *my*
Grubber shop, it is home time.
Monkey sings —

We love to be with you, we three.

Do please now and then

Come and see us again,

The Giraffe, and the Pelly and me.

Before You Read

1 Look at the cover.
What kind of story is this? Why?

a a funny story
b a sad story
c a true story
d an exciting story

2 What things *don't* you usually find in a house?

windows

doors

trees

baths

rivers

bicycles

sinks

long ladders

police cars

elephants

After You Read

1 **What do they eat in the story? Match.**

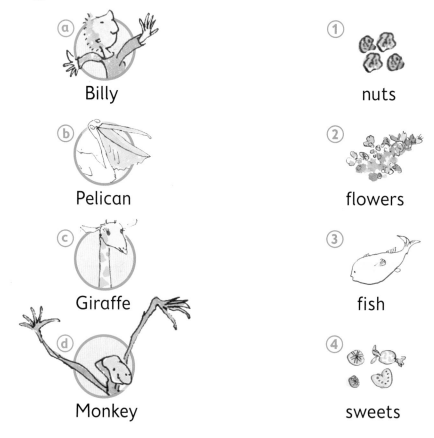

ⓐ Billy

ⓑ Pelican

ⓒ Giraffe

ⓓ Monkey

① nuts

② flowers

③ fish

④ sweets

2 **Read and write Yes (Y) or No (N).**

a Billy lives in the old house.

b Giraffe needs a tall door.

c The animals clean shoes.

d Monkey cleans windows.

e The Duke has a small house.

f The thief takes the purple flowers.

g The Duke catches the thief.

h Billy opens a sweet shop.